Hi, I'm Covi and I'm really pleased to meet you!
Please read me every time that you are feeling blue.
Do you like counting dinosaurs instead of counting sheep?
Then let me cheer you up! And help you go to sleep...

Mummy said, 'We must stay at home,'
and Emily was sad.
She missed her school and teachers;
she missed Granny and her Dad.
She could not go out to the park,
nor see her best friend Mo.
'When will things go back to normal?'
But mummy did not know...

Emily sat by her bedroom window,
looking down on to the street,
There were no cars or delivery vans,
no neighbours chatting as they meet.
But then she spied the strangest sight!
It made her blink and roar –
For there upon the village green was a little green dinosaur...!

Emily's mummy rushed straight in the room,
'Emily, what IS the drama?'
The little girl shouted with delight,
'Look! Can you see him, Mama?'
Her mother looked but all she saw was their
pussycat called Tilly.
'Emily,' she declared, 'it is time for bed,
I think you're being silly!'

Emily was snoring loudly when she heard
noise outside her house,
She snuck downstairs to check it out,
tiptoeing as quietly as a mouse.
She squealed, 'It's you! I didn't make it up!
Hip Hip Hip Hurrah!'
The little green stranger was back,
and he was sitting on their car!

'Hi, my name is Covi,' the little green dinosaur said,
'And I'm really pleased to meet you.
Is your name Oskar or is it Fred?'
Emily giggled as she replied, 'NO, silly I am a GIRL!'
'You can tell by the way I dance,' she said
and spun around in a twirl.

The little girl told the dinosaur,
'I'm Emily and I'm pleased to meet you.'
'I'm happy you said that,' he said,
'grown-ups think I want to EAT you!'
They chatted for a little while and he told her why he came,
'Because people must stay inside,' he said,
'which really is a shame.'

'But we all want you to stay safe,'
Covi told her with a sigh.
'You need to help the world get better,
it's really best you try.
AND when the people stay inside,
the earth can start to glow!
Stars get bright, the air is clean –
the rainforests and coral grow!'

'The mermaids will go back to the seas,
the fairies can fly again!
Giants and unicorns can come back too,
for they are scared of men.
The strange noises and the rushing around had sent them
all away,
But now the earth is quieter,
they are coming out to play!'

'Creatures can go to the park when nobody's there
and play upon the swings,
My friends can run around in the streets and do all sorts of things!
If somebody is living alone and has nothing left to eat,
I can pop along to the shops and pick them up a tasty treat!'

'So please stay safe, my little one,
this is only for a while,
And if you're sad I will visit you,'
Covi promised with a smile.
They talked for a while and had some fun,
then Emily started yawning.
'It's time for bed now, Emily, good night.
I'll see you in the morning.'

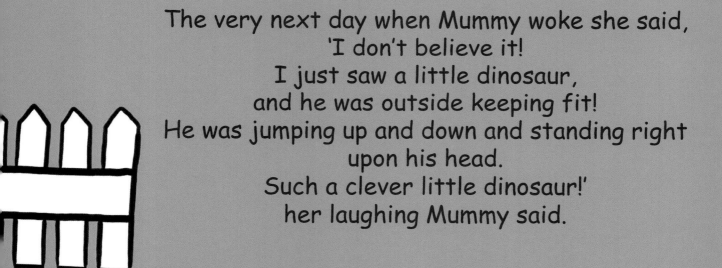

The very next day when Mummy woke she said,
'I don't believe it!
I just saw a little dinosaur,
and he was outside keeping fit!
He was jumping up and down and standing right
upon his head.
Such a clever little dinosaur!'
her laughing Mummy said.

Covi came to see Emily and her friends many times that year,
Until one day doors opened up and Mummy said,
'The coast is clear!'
Emily would miss her funny green friend but she never would forget,
How he came to comfort the children,
so that they would not fret.

One day when she was all grown up,
Emily switched on the telly
And she couldn't believe her eyes,
for there was Covi eating jelly!
He was featured in a TV show –
it seems he was a star!
That same little green dinosaur
she found sitting on their car.

Emily turned to her own little girl and told her of
the special friend,
Whom she had met when the world was shut,
and how it came right in the end.
The sky and the earth had time to heal
and how all the animals had danced,
How the fairies flew, the giants stomped
and the unicorns had pranced!

And when all the people came back –
let out of their homes at last –
They had changed their ways and slowed
right down,
not taking life so fast.
They loved their friends and families
and spent more time having fun,
They were happy and contented just to
be sitting in the sun.

And so sometimes when things seem hard
and you want to sit and cry,
Just think about the flowers that bloom,
and the sun up in the sky,
The birds that fly, the bees that hum
and the bread upon your table;
Smile, and thank a little dinosaur,
for bringing you this fable.

Thank you to our incredible illustrators Chay & Kaitlyn who brought our little 'Covi' to life.

Susie Cullen

You can now keep in touch with 'Covi' via Facebook, Twitter and Instagram and watch lovely video readings of the stories on YouTube.

Just search 'Covi, the little green dinosaur'!

Thank you to the children of Harlington for sharing their wonderful 'Covi' drawings with us. If you would like free 'Covi' colouring sheets, pop over to our social media channels and say hi!

Print book format & design by
Sunil Nissanka Amarasinghe
(Top Rated freelancer on Upwork)
Contact: sumudamar@gmail.com

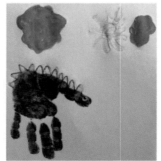

Printed in Great Britain
by Amazon